ZOE DISCOVERS
HANUKKAH
AT
CHRISTMAS

ISBN: 9798778490727

Then came Hanukkah; it was winter in Jerusalem. Yeshua was walking in the Temple around Solomon's Colonnade.

John 10:22-23

DEDICATION

This book is dedicated to granddaughter Isabella Jaworowicz.

Her loving attitude, especial toward children is an inspiration. She celebrates Hanukkah with me every year. This year (2021) she came to stay while I finished this book and to comfort me since I am alone.

God bless you, Bella.

FOREWORD

This book was written and edited during a period of great difficulty. My husband, Ron, was in the hospital suffering repeated lung injuries through a series of treatments, setbacks, and recoveries. There were prayers being said for him all over the world. He fought bravely for three months until a final lung injury made another recovery impossible. Ron graduated to heaven in October 2021. We would have celebrated our 35th wedding anniversary in December of the same year.

His ardent desire was to promote and share these books with everyone (if you were on his list, you know!) Christian, Jew, Messianic, or Atheist. Even from his hospital bed he was sharing the launch of the Fall feasts books (Rosh Hashana, Yom Kippur, and Sukkot) in September.

Therefore, after his passing, I knew without question this book would be the ONE THING he would want me to accomplish. So in loving memory of my best friend in the world, I present *Zoe Discovers Hanukkah at Christmas*.

This holiday is about dedication. Dedication to the LORD in the midst of difficult, painful circumstances is something we all have to deal with, eventually. May this story of love, faith, and perseverance spur you on to good works and encourage you to press on toward the goal of the upward call of Messiah.

Rene Annette Wallace

Master of Practical Theology

Author and Teacher

www.entertheblessings.com

Zoe loved living in a pretty house with Mommy and Daddy and her little brother, Zack.
After Thanksgiving every year, Daddy always got the Christmas lights out of the rafters in the garage.

One day after school, Zoe put on a warm winter sweater because it was getting cold outside. She went with Daddy to the garage to find the ladder and get the decorations. The ladder was gone! Then he remembered he loaned it to a friend. Daddy said to Zoe, "Let's go next-door and see if Zhava's dad, Mr. Kaplan, can loan me a ladder."

Zoe and Daddy knocked on the door, and Zhava's daddy answered. The daddies and the girls all walked together to Zhava's garage.

"What is your Daddy doing with the ladder?" Zhava asked. Zoe said, "We are hanging Christmas lights today. We always do that after Thanksgiving. Are you putting up Christmas lights?"

Zhava crunched her eyebrows and answered, "I don't think so. We are lighting menorahs." Zoe asked, "What's a menorah?" Zhava said, "Want to come, and see? We have them in our living room!" So, Zoe asked Daddy and he said she could go look at the menorahs.

Zhava had five menorahs. One was big and gold and shiny. One was shaped like a half star, one was made from wood and metal pieces glued together, and the others were smaller and silver colored. Zhava said, "We light these for Hanukkah. Every night we light an extra candle. We light them for eight nights in a row."

Zoe counted the candles in one of the menorahs and asked, "Why do they have nine candle holders?" "One candle is special; it is the SHAMASH or "servant" candle. We have to light all the other candles with the servant candle." Zhava replied.

"My mommy and daddy told me it's like the light of Messiah Yeshua, the Servant. When he was here, he said, 'I am the light of the world.' Hanukkah is the festival of lights and Yeshua is our light!" Zoe thought about that and remembered the song "This Little Light of Mine." She started humming.

It was time to go home, so Zoe said, "Thank you for showing me your menorahs. They must be pretty when they are all lit up." And Zhava said, "We will be lighting them tomorrow for the eighth night. Do you want to come over and see?" Zoe was excited, "Yes! I will ask Mommy and Daddy."

When Zoe got home, she told Zack all about the beautiful menorahs. Zack wanted to see them too. Mommy heard them talking and said, "Zoe and Zack, you are going to see them! We have been invited next door tomorrow for Hanukkah!" Zack smiled really big and started jumping up and down. Zoe laughed. Zack was so funny!

The next night, Daddy, Mommy, Zoe, and Zack walked over to the neighbor's house. Zhava's mom looked so pretty, and Zoe's mom made her special salad with walnuts. Mr. and Mrs. Kaplan were so kind and always wanted to share. Zoe was so happy and excited to learn about another holiday!

For dinner, Mrs. Kaplan made some special potato pancakes and she explained they were called LATKES. They were so yummy, Zoe wanted to eat them all! After dinner, everyone went to the living room and sat down around the menorahs on the table. Zhava's house had pretty blue and silver decorations all around. When they all sat down, Mr. Kaplan told a story.

"A long, long time ago, an evil ruler tried to take over the land of Israel where the Hebrew people lived and worshiped God. The evil ruler would not let the Hebrew people read the scriptures or celebrate the holy days that God had commanded. The ruler even made the soldiers destroy the holy place of God."

"Some strong priests named the Maccabees fought back against the evil ruler and his strong army and they won! It was a miracle!"

He continued, "After they defeated the mean ruler and his army, the Maccabees cleaned and rededicated the holy place and the holy items to God, like the giant Temple menorah. After the war, the menorah needed oil and the Rabbis say the little bit of oil that was left kept the menorah lit for eight days while messengers went to get fresh oil!"

"One thing we remember at this season is the day Messiah walked in the Temple during The Feast of Dedication. He was answering the question, 'Are you the Messiah?'
And He answered, 'I do the works of the Father.'"
The servant candle reminds us of our Messiah who came to be the servant of all. We, too, should serve others with love. And finally, this holiday of dedication reminds us every year to rededicate our lives to God."

Then, Mr. Kaplan looked at his wife and said, "Honey, is it time to light the candles?"

And Mrs. Kaplan answered, "Yes!"

So, the three children each had their own menorah and the parents had to share. Zoe thought it was fun to have her very own!

They lit the servant candle and Mrs. Kaplan said a blessing in Hebrew. Zoe didn't understand the Hebrew words, but Mrs. Kaplan repeated the blessing in English.

She said, "Blessed are you, Lord our God, King of the Universe ..."

Zoe thought. "How big God is to be the King of all the planets and stars in the sky!"

Then Mrs. Kaplan gave everyone jelly donuts. They were called SUFGANIYOT. It was a funny name that sounded like "soup and a goat!" They were even better than the latkes! Mommy said Zoe and Zach could have one. The children played a game called DREIDEL with chocolate coins called GELT and using spinning tops called DREIDELS!

When they were leaving, Mrs. Taylor invited the Kaplans over for Christmas. Zoe was so happy to learn about Hanukkah and Jesus and laugh and play with Zhava.

Zoe hugged Zhava and said, "See you at Christmas! Thank you for showing me Jesus in Hanukkah. We will be friends for a long time!"

Zhava smiled, "Yes! We will."

Thank you for joining us on this journey of discovery with Zoe and Zhava. (Jayden and Han will be back next time.)

If you and your child (or grandchild) enjoyed this story, PLEASE go to Amazon and post a few lines about what you liked in a review. This will enable more people to experience the joy of the Jewish holidays and better understand the Jewish roots of our Christian faith.

AND, sign up for free resources, like a FREE guide on how to use this book at www.EnterTheBlessings.com

May you walk ever closer to God through the Feasts of the Lord.

SUBSCRIBE:

Although we can't visit Israel (as of publication), you can still get the taste, smell, and experience of Israel in your own home! Subscribe to ARTZA BOXES! (Cancel anytime, but I don't think you will! I love mine.)
I am an affiliate, which means I will make a little bit of money if you sign up! https://bit.ly/36ZFuZe Use my coupon code ARTZARENEWALLACE for a discount!

SIGN-UP:

Go to www.entertheblessings.com JOIN THE MOVEMENT to receive free resources and monthly updates about our new books.

DONATE:

The enemies of Israel are burning down forests with balloons. Please consider planting a tree. For a $50 donation to our non-profit we will plant a tree and send you a certificate in your name.
Go to www.entertheblessings.com (Bless Israel — Plant a Tree)

Made in the USA
Monee, IL
02 December 2024

72022762R00017